PRiNCE
NOT·SO
CHARMiNG

The Prince Not-So Charming series

Once Upon a Prank

Her Royal Slyness

The Dork Knight

Happily Ever Laughter

Toad You So!

Wild Wild Quest

PRINCE NOT-SO CHARMING

Wild Wild Quest

Roy L. Hinuss

Illustrated by Matt Hunt

[Imprint]
MAKE YOUR MARK

New York

[Imprint]
MAKE YOUR MARK

A part of Macmillan Publishing Group, LLC
175 Fifth Avenue, New York, NY 10010

PRINCE NOT-SO CHARMING: WILD WILD QUEST. Copyright © 2019 by
Imprint. All rights reserved. Printed in the United States of America by
LSC Communications, Harrisonburg, Virginia.

Library of Congress Cataloging-in-Publication Data is available.

ISBN 978-1-250-14248-1 (paperback) / ISBN 978-1-250-14247-4 (ebook)

Our books may be purchased in bulk for promotional, educational, or
business use. Please contact your local bookseller or the Macmillan
Corporate and Premium Sales Department at (800) 221-7945 ext. 5442 or
by email at MacmillanSpecialMarkets@macmillan.com.

Book design by Ellen Duda

Illustrations by Matt Hunt

Imprint logo designed by Amanda Spielman

First edition, 2019

1   3   5   7   9   10   8   6   4   2

mackids.com

Book thieves beware. You have been hexed!
Confused? Befuddled? Stumped? Perplexed?
Let me explain. This book you took
Bewitched yer butt, you dirty crook.
This hex will make you cry and wail.
You'll ouch and ache from nose to tail.
All things you own will fall apart.
And vanish like a wispy fart.
All things "just so" will go so wrong.
Your life will be just one sad song.
Want to escape? There's just one way:
This hex will vanish once you *pay*!

For Katie. Because she's awesome.

CHAPTER 1

Prince Carlos Charles Charming coughed and wheezed. He sniffed and hacked. He moaned and groaned and gritted his teeth in agony.

"I have a stomachache!" he cried. "A sore throat! A fever! The flu! A broken leg! Mad cow disease!"

King Carmine listened patiently to Carlos's list of many ailments. He put a gentle hand on the boy's shoulder. "I'm sorry, son," he said, "but you're going to the opera."

"But I can't!" Carlos gasped. "I'm dyyy-yyyyyying!"

"You are not dying," the king said. "And you have to go. Members of the royal family are *required* to go to cultural events."

"Even to the opera?!" Carlos sputtered.

"*Especially* to the opera," the king said.

"Why?"

The king rubbed his eyes as if they hurt. "Because it makes your mother very happy," he replied.

◆　◆　◆

On stage, a large woman wearing a horned helmet howled a long, shrill, wobbly note. Her mouth was open so wide that Carlos thought he could almost see down to her large intestines.

The note jabbed at Carlos's eardrums, thumped against his forehead, and tap-danced up and down his spine.

This is the most terrible thing I have ever heard, he thought.

Then a dozen other singers wandered on-stage. All of them howled long, shrill, wobbly notes, too.

Scratch that, Carlos thought. *THIS is the most terrible thing I have ever heard.*

Carlos did his best to block out the wall of sound. But it wasn't easy.

Not easy at all.

Carlos peeked at his father. The king wore a frown on his tan, lined face. King Carmine's face was often frowny, even when he wasn't in a frowny mood, but Carlos could tell that *this* frown was the real deal.

Queen Cora, on the other hand, was so excited that she could barely keep still. She bounced and jiggled happily in her seat. A smile stretched across her wide, round face.

"Oh, Carmine, isn't the soprano superb?" she whispered in the king's ear. "Such talent, such passion! Such talented passion!"

"Mm," the king replied.

Carlos whispered in the king's other ear, "Is it almost over?"

"Not even close," the king whispered back a little sadly.

Carlos slumped in his seat.

His mind soon began to wander. When

Carlos's mind wandered, it almost always wandered to the same place: jestering.

Carlos was the prince of the happy and peaceful land of Faraway Kingdom—but his *passion* was jestering. Carlos was widely considered to be one of the best jesters on the continent. His fart jokes made audiences roar with laughter. His acrobatics made them cheer. His musical skills made their toes tap. His juggling mastery earned him first-prize honors at the International Jester Juggle-A-Thon. His photo had even appeared on the cover of *Jester Beat* magazine.

So as the opera went on (and on and on),

Carlos's mind pondered a jester-y brainteaser that had been rattling around in his brain all day.

"A jester's mind must always be nimble and creative," Jack the Jester had told Carlos that morning. Jack was the official jester of the Charming Royal Family. He was also Carlos's friend and teacher. "So, kiddo, here's a puzzle for you to solve."

The question Jack posed seemed simple enough: "What's at the end of a rainbow?"

"A pot of gold," Carlos had guessed.

"Nope," Jack had replied.

Nope?! Carlos had thought. *How can that be a "nope"?*

Carlos crinkled his eyebrows in deep thought. But his eyebrow crinkles didn't help. He couldn't come up with another answer.

"Remember, young'un," Jack had told him, "brainteasers always make sense, but they only make sense in a tricky way."

What's at the end of a rainbow? Carlos thought. He closed his eyes in concentration. He no longer heard the opera. Every bit of his attention was now focused on solving that riddle. He thought about the question very carefully.

What's at the end of a rainbow?

He examined each word in his mind.

What's . . . at . . . the . . . end . . . of . . . a . . . rainbow?

He wondered how the words could make sense in a tricky way.

What's at the end . . .

His eyes shot open. In a flash, the answer sprang to his lips.

"*W!*" Carlos shouted as he jumped to his feet. "A *W* IS AT THE END OF—"

The Faraway Kingdom Opera House suddenly fell very silent.

The singers stopped singing.

Hundreds of heads turned. (His mom and dad were two of those turning heads.)

Everyone stared at Carlos in alarm.

Carlos cleared his throat. He felt his face get hot. "A *W* is at the end of a *rainbow*," he explained. He cleared his throat again. "Because it's the last letter of the word."

Wasting no time, King Carmine took command of the situation. (After all, that's what good kings are supposed to do.) He stood and bowed to the stunned opera singers. He then addressed the audience. "Ladies and gentlemen. I apologize for the outburst. My son is not feeling well today. He has recently contracted . . ."

"Mad cow disease!" Carlos said, trying to be helpful.

The king did *not* find that helpful. "Shush," he whispered.

Before the king could come up with a plausible illness, the opera house's sound system crackled to life:

**Calling His Majesty King Carmine!
Calling His Majesty King Carmine!
Please report to the lobby for an
Emergency King Conference!**

The crowd gasped. A King Conference was
a very important meeting between two kings.
An *Emergency* King Conference was a super-
duper, holy-schmoley, impossibly supersized
important meeting between two kings.

So it was kind of a big deal.

Emergency King Conferences hardly *ever*
happened. And no king ever *wanted* them to
happen, because they usually meant that a
terrible, horrible something had happened.

And terrible, horrible somethings are both terrible and horrible.

"Come with me, son," the king whispered.

Carlos's stomach did a quick backflip.

"What? Why?" Carlos whispered. "I don't want to deal with terrible, horrible somethings."

"Sometimes a prince has to deal with terrible, horrible somethings," the king said.

"Even if the prince has mad cow disease?" Carlos asked.

The king raised an impatient eyebrow. "*Especially* if the prince has mad cow disease," he replied.

CHAPTER 2

"CARMINE!"

The man waiting in the lobby looked very kingly. He was tall and muscular. He stood very straight. He was draped in red velvet. His shaved, ebony head gleamed in the light from an overhead chandelier. Carlos recognized the man immediately. He was King

Martin McMoots, the ever-cheerful ruler of the nearby kingdom of Ever-After Land.

But King Martin was not cheerful now. His forehead was crinkled with lines of worry. His mouth was twisted into a terrible frown. Carlos had never seen King Martin frown before. It was unsettling.

King Carmine extended his hand in friendship. "Martin, what's the matter?"

Martin took Carmine's hand and shook it. (Martin was too strong and too worried to notice that he was shaking the rest of Carmine, too.)

"I am so sorry to interrupt your night

out," King Martin said, "but something ter-rible and horrible has happened!"

King Carmine pried his hand from Mar-tin's grip. "What is it?"

"My wonderful son, Prince Gilbert, is missing!" King Martin said.

Carlos knew Prince Gilbert very well. He was the oh-so-perfect prince of Ever-After Land. If you looked up the word *prince* in the dictionary, you'd see Prince Gilbert's picture. If you looked up the word *perfect* in the dictionary, you'd find Prince Gilbert's picture there, too.

Carlos thought Prince Gilbert was *too* perfect. Prince Gilbert could sword fight, joust, rescue maidens, lead armies, and slay giants. Prince Gilbert was also brave and brilliant and handsome and patient and polite and kind and confident and modest.

See? Perfect.

That was why Carlos couldn't believe his ears. A prince as perfect as Gilbert would not go missing. "I don't believe it," Carlos said.

"I can hardly believe it myself," King Martin moaned. "But it's true! Gilbert set out to fulfill a royal quest. He sailed upon the Salty Sea to find the Be-Sworded Stone."

"The Be-*Whated What*?" Carlos asked.

"The Be-Sworded Stone," King Martin said. "It's a stone. With a sword stuck in it."

"So it's called the Be-Sworded Stone because the sword be in the stone?" Carlos asked.

"Yes," King Martin said.

"That's terrible grammar," Carlos said.

"Yes," King Martin agreed. "The prophecy of the Be-Sworded Stone goes like this: 'Whosoever discovers the sword in the Be-Sworded Stone and takes it home will bring endless joy to his or her kingdom!'"

"*Whosoever* is a word?" Carlos asked.

"Apparently so," King Martin replied. "Gilbert set out on this quest three weeks ago. And he's vanished without a trace! I fear that he has faced a tragedy! Maybe his boat sank! Or maybe he was attacked by pirates, scalawags, and no-goodniks!"

King Carmine put a gentle hand on King Martin's shoulder. "We don't know that, Martin. Maybe Gilbert's just having trouble pulling the sword out of the stone."

Martin was insulted by the very idea. "Not my Gilbert!" he protested. "He's too perfectly princely to struggle with a simple sword. My kingly intuition tells me that a darkness has fallen over my beloved son. He needs to be rescued!"

"Then I'll rescue him!" someone said.

That someone was Princess Pinky, Prince Gilbert's younger sister and Carlos's best friend. Pinky poked her head out from behind the opera house's candy counter. Her cheeks were stuffed with Milk Duds. "I told you I'd rescue him, Dad. Geez! Why are we even here?"

King Martin trembled with impatience. "We are here, young lady, because you don't know the first thing about rescuing. All you do all day is draw pictures in that silly sketchbook of yours."

That wasn't true. Pinky also used oil paints and sculpted things with clay. Pinky was passionate about art the same way Carlos was passionate about jestering. Pinky's usual outfit was a pair of paint-splattered overalls. Since she was at the opera house with her father, however, she was wearing a dress. Pinky did not like wearing dresses.

"I can still rescue him!" Pinky grumped, futzing with the dress's neckline.

"How?" King Martin asked.

"I'll figure it out," she said. "How hard could it be?"

"It could be *very* hard!" King Martin exclaimed. (Worried people sometimes exclaim too much.) "That's why I called this Emergency King Conference! I need help from an *expert*. Gilbert helped train Prince Carlos. Therefore, Carlos must possess Gilbert's expert rescuing skills."

Not necessarily, Carlos thought.

King Martin turned to King Carmine. "This is why I'm here. I'm begging you, Carmine. I'm on my knees."

King Martin was not on his knees.

"That is, I *would* be on my knees if I didn't have that runner's injury," King Martin added. "You know the injury I'm talking about?"

"Not really, no," King Carmine said. "But

that doesn't matter. What do you want from me, Martin?"

"I want to borrow your son," King Martin said. "That is, I was hoping your son could rescue my son."

And there it was: the terrible and horrible something. Carlos decided that he really *hated* Emergency King Conferences.

"I see." King Carmine considered King Martin's words very carefully. "Well, I think a decision like that should be made by Carlos."

In that moment, Carlos's and Pinky's eyes met.

Pinky looked angry. She wasn't angry at

Carlos. She was angry because her dad didn't trust her with the rescue. She was angry because her dad yelled at her. She was angry because her dad called her sketchbook "silly."

She was also angry because Carlos had *no* rescuing experience.

Pinky *did* have rescuing experience; once upon a time, she had rescued Carlos from falling off the side of the Tallest Tower!

So Pinky was *very* angry.

Carlos could see that Pinky was very angry. He could also see *why* Pinky was very angry. Best friends understand things like that.

So Carlos made his decision. "Okay, I'll rescue Gilbert," he said.

"Wonderful!" King Martin cried.

"But *only* if Pinky can come with me," Carlos said.

"WHAT?!" King Martin bellowed.

Pinky's anger suddenly vanished. Her eyes sparkled with excitement. A smile stretched across her face.

"I think your daughter is a very good rescuer," Carlos said.

"You do?" King Martin asked.

"Yes," Carlos said.

"Really?" King Martin asked.

"Yes," Carlos said.

"Pinky?" King Martin asked.

"Yes!" Carlos said. "And I should know, because I was trained by Prince Gilbert!"

King Martin considered this. "That's true. You *would* know. Gilbert trained you! You're an expert rescuer!"

"Everything will work out just fine," Carlos said confidently.

But as he said it, an *un*confident thought flashed through Carlos's mind:

If perfect Gilbert can't rescue himself, how am I supposed to rescue him?

Then Carlos thought of something else:

And if I can't rescue him, who the heck is going to rescue me?

CHAPTER 3

Carlos sat on the shore of the Salty Sea, staring at charts and maps. Pinky sat next to him, flipping through a small black journal.

"Here it is!" she announced, tapping a page with her finger. "I know exactly where Gilbert went. According to his research, the Be-Sworded Stone is on Dessert Island."

Carlos's eyes focused on the page. "We have to go to a desert island? Oh, no."

"Not a *desert* island," Pinky said. "*Dessert* Island! It's supposed to be an amazing place. On Dessert Island, ice cream grows on trees."

Carlos raised a suspicious eyebrow. "Ice cream does not grow on trees."

"On Dessert Island it does," Pinky said. "On Dessert Island we can eat all the ice cream we want."

Pinky didn't say this very loudly, but she said it loudly enough.

Carlos immediately heard the thumpita-thumpitas of galloping footsteps. A dragon the size of a rhinoceros burst through a tall patch of beach grass and bounded to the water's edge. He joyously flopped onto the sand beside Carlos and Pinky.

He was Smudge, Faraway Kingdom's

resident dragon. "Oh, hai, CC! Hai, Pinky!"
he chirped.

Smudge looked very much like every
other dragon that lurked in the forests
throughout the continent. He had scaly

skin, a long neck, sharp fangs, and bat-like wings.

But Smudge did not act like every other dragon. Unlike other dragons, Smudge was not vicious and ferocious. Smudge liked cuddles and kisses. He did not set fire to villages or eat people. Instead, Smudge preferred to cool his fiery breath by eating ice cream.

Lots and lots of ice cream.

"Are you guys getting ready to go someplace?" Smudge asked. "'Cause I wanna go wherever it is you're going."

Carlos smirked. "Oh, really?"

"Yuh-huh!" Smudge said with a big nod. "And I don't even need to know *where* you're going. Because being with my bestest friends is the *only* thing in the world that matters. So even if you're going to a nasty, awful, stinky place, I will go with you! To help!"

"Wow." Pinky was smiling, too. "You'd do that for us?"

"Oh, yes!" Smudge said. "I will help you with the stuff at the place where I don't know where you're going."

"You didn't hear Pinky say where we're going?" Carlos asked.

"Nuh-uh," Smudge said.

"Or what grows on the trees there?" Pinky added.

"It is a mystery to me," Smudge said.

"Wow. Smudge is such a loyal friend," Pinky said.

"And dedicated," Carlos agreed.

"And hungry," Smudge added.

◆ ◆ ◆

Later that morning, Carlos, Pinky, and Smudge raised the sail on their tiny sloop—a sailboat with a single mast—and let the wind push them out to sea.

Knowing that the journey to Dessert Island was going to be a long one, Carlos had asked Jack for a few brainteasers to keep his mind busy. The old jester was happy to write out some for him. Carlos leaned against the sloop's mast and read the question at the top of the page. *Seven months of the year have thirty-one days. How many have twenty-eight?*

Carlos's first instinct was to say "one," because February was the only month of the year that was twenty-eight days long. But Carlos was starting to get the hang of how brainteasers worked. He needed to think about how the question made sense in a tricky way.

Seven months of the year have thirty-one days.
How many have twenty-eight?

He studied every word.

Seven months of the year have thirty-one days.
How many have twenty-eight?

Carlos smiled.

The brainteaser wasn't asking how many months were twenty-eight days long. The brainteaser was asking how many months *had* twenty-eight days. Since every month was at least twenty-eight days long . . .

"*All* twelve months have twenty-eight days!" Carlos shouted.

"What?" Pinky asked. She was seated next to the sloop's rudder.

39

"Oh, sorry," Carlos said. "I guess I have a bad habit of yelling the answers to brainteasers."

"You have brainteasers?" Pinky asked. "Read me one."

"Okay," Carlos ran his finger down the page but was soon distracted by Smudge. The dragon was sitting next to him, staring into the water and making flappy motions with his paws.

"What'cha doing, Smudge?" Carlos asked.

"Looking for sea monsters."

"Why are you flapping your hands like that?" Carlos asked.

"I'm trying to say hi to sea monsters."

Carlos's stomach twitched. "Do you see any sea monsters?"

"No," Smudge said, a little disappointed.

"Come on!" Pinky called. "Gimme a brainteaser!"

"Okay," Carlos replied. "Hey, Smudge, do you want to hear a brainteaser?"

Smudge pulled his gaze away from the water. "Oh, I don't like teasing. A long time ago, the other dragons teased me because I didn't wanna set villages on fire with my hot bref. And it hurt my feelings."

"No, not that kind of teasing, Smudge," Carlos said. He scratched the scales under the dragon's chin. "I would *never* tease you like that. This is a *brain*teaser."

Smudge considered this. "I don't think my brain would like to be teased, either," he said.

"Carlos, I'm growing old here!" Pinky called.

"Oh, sorry!" Carlos called back. He selected a random question and read it loud enough for Pinky to hear. "'A butcher is six feet tall and has a shoe size of twelve. What does he weigh?'"

"How should I know?" Pinky said. "Is he fat?"

"It doesn't say," Carlos replied.

"Is there a picture of him?" Pinky asked.

"No," Carlos said.

"Then how am I supposed to get it?" Pinky said. "There isn't enough information."

"We should be able to get the answer with the information we have," Carlos said. But he was having trouble with this brainteaser, too.

"So he's six feet . . ." Pinky muttered. "Size twelve shoes . . ."

Carlos read the question aloud again. "'A butcher is six feet tall and has a shoe size of twelve. What does he weigh?'"

"Meat," Smudge replied.

"Meat?!" Pinky asked.

"Meat!" Carlos exclaimed. "Of course! The question isn't asking *how much* the butcher weighs. It's asking *what* the butcher weighs. And butchers weigh meat! Smudge, how did you know that?"

"I'm very good with questions about food,"
Smudge replied.

◆　◆　◆

For the next hour, the wind blew cheerily.
Pinky steered the boat and read brainteasers
at the same time.

"'What gets wet when drying?'" Pinky
asked.

"A towel," Carlos replied.

Pinky threw up her hands. "How do you
solve these things so dang fast?"

"Practice, I guess," Carlos said.

"Okay." Pinky scanned the questions for

a tricky one. "Ah! Let's see how well you do with *this* one, smarty-pants: 'What's full of holes but holds water?'"

Carlos silently pondered the question for a long moment.

"A sponge," he replied.

"Dangit!" Pinky shouted.

◆ ◆ ◆

Pinky's pencil flew across the surface of her sketchbook. In a few quick, curly lines, she made the churning waves of the Salty Sea come alive on the page.

"Do you want to hear another brain-teaser?" Carlos asked. He was at the rudder now.

"No," she replied. "My brain has been teased enough."

"I told you, CC!" Smudge scolded. "Brains don't like to be teased!"

"Do you want to hear a brainteaser, Smudge?"

"No, I am too busy trying to say hi to sea monsters." Smudge waved down at the waves.

"Don't you know that sea monsters *eat* sailors?" Carlos asked.

"I'm sure some of them don't," Smudge replied.

◆ ◆ ◆

"Are we there yet?" Smudge asked. My tummy's got the grumbles."

Pinky was back at the rudder. "We still have a long way to go," she said.

"Oh, poop," Smudge grouched. "If I knew that Dessert Island was so far, I woulda brought fudge-ickles with me."

"Well, maybe I can help," Carlos said with a little smile. He reached under the seat and pulled out a Styrofoam cooler. He opened the lid.

And Smudge went bananas.

"FUDGE-ICKLES! YOU BROUGHT ME FUDGE-ICKLES!" Smudge squealed.

"I heard rumors that you like them," Carlos said.

"I LOOOOVE THEM!" Smudge hopped and skipped with delight, making the sloop wobble from side to side.

"Whoa!" Pinky called out. "You're going to tip us over!"

Actually, Smudge's hopping and skipping wasn't enough to tip the boat over. But when Smudge got excited, he sometimes did *more* than hop and skip.

Smudge snatched a fudgesickle from the cooler.

As he did so, a happy, excited fireball shot from his mouth.

BAWOOSH!

"Smudge!" Carlos cried. "NO!"

But it was too late. In a flash, the sloop's sail burst into flames.

CHAPTER 4

It didn't take much time for Carlos, Pinky, and Smudge to put out the fire. Unfortunately, the fire took even less time to turn the sail to ash.

Smudge's lower lip began to quiver. "I'm sorry."

"It's okay," Carlos replied.

But Carlos knew it really wasn't okay. A sailboat without a sail was a real problem. The wind was useless to them now. The sloop couldn't move forward.

◆ ◆ ◆

The boat bobbed up and down in the waves. Carlos didn't know how long they had been bobbing, but he guessed it was at least a couple of hours.

Carlos scanned the horizon. There was no sign of land in any direction.

Smudge looked like he was about to cry. "I wish I could control my hot bref better!"

"Oh, Smudge," Carlos said. "Don't worry. We'll get out of this somehow." He gave the dragon a hug. Smudge hugged him back, wiping his moist dragon snout on Carlos's shirt.

Ew, Carlos thought.

"We'll be fine, Smudge," Carlos said. "Isn't that right, Pinky?"

Pinky didn't respond.

In fact, she hadn't said much of anything since the fire.

Pinky had her back to Carlos and Smudge. She stared out at the water.

"Pinky?" Carlos called.

"What?" she said.

"Smudge is very upset," Carlos explained. "And I was telling him that this is nothing to worry about. Isn't that right?"

Pinky's voice suddenly oozed with fake enthusiasm. "Oh! Absolutely! Nothing to worry about." Carlos still couldn't see Pinky's face, but it sounded like she was speaking through gritted teeth. "This is just *delightful*. This is *tons* of fun. Look at all the *fun* we're having!"

Then Pinky added a ferocious "YIPPEE!"

It was the "yippee" that made Smudge burst into tears.

"I knew it!" Smudge howled, choking on snotty sniffles. "I ruined our royal quest!"

Carlos hugged Smudge even tighter than before.

Now it was Carlos's turn to speak through gritted teeth. "PINKY! Why are you being so

mean to Smudge? It was just a little accident!"

Pinky whirled around. Carlos was shocked
to see tears streaming down her cheeks. "A
'little accident'?" she roared. "Well, that
'little accident' will keep us from rescuing
Gilbert!"

Then Pinky *really* began to cry.

Smudge *really* began to cry, too.

Ugh. Too much crying, Carlos thought.

It was up to Carlos to calm things down.

He understood why Pinky was crying. Best friends understand things like this.

"I understand," Carlos said. "You're worried about Gilbert."

"Are you serious? I'm not worried about Gilbert!" Pinky yelled. "I can't *stand* Gilbert!"

Huh. Maybe best friends *didn't* understand things like this.

"Then why the heck are you crying?" Carlos asked.

"I am *not* crying!" Pinky said, wiping her eyes.

"You look like you're crying," Carlos said.

"Well, I'm NOT!" cried Pinky.

"I'm crying," cried Smudge.

"I know you're crying, Smudge," Carlos said. And he hugged the dragon even tighter.

No one said anything for a long time after that. And that was fine with Carlos. He just sat very still, listening to Pinky and Smudge sniffle.

When Pinky spoke again, she wasn't nearly as sad or as angry as before. She sounded tired. "For my *entire* life, I have been compared to my brother. Every day I hear about how wonderful Gilbert is. 'Gilbert can do this. Gilbert can do that. Gilbert can do *anything*!'"

"Come on. That can't be true," Carlos said.

"Oh, it's true," she said. "Gilbert doesn't waste his time drawing pictures. Gilbert doesn't wear dirty overalls. Gilbert doesn't eat his soup with a fork. Or stay up late. Or play in the mud. Or leave his crown out in the rain. Because Gilbert is *perfect*!"

Smudge wiped away a dragon tear and listened very carefully.

"So when perfect Gilbert disappeared, I

saw my chance," Pinky said. "I'd rescue him. I'd be a hero. I'd out-perfect the perfect prince! And *everyone* would know it."

She allowed herself to smile a little. "And it would be soooo cool."

Then Pinky pointed to the charred sail. "And *this* is what my rescue looks like. Now we need someone to rescue *us*."

Pinky sighed. She flopped onto one of the sloop's benches. "It's just so . . ."

"Poop stinky," said Smudge. "I understand how you feel, Pinky. My older sisters were perfect. They would eat villagers. They'd eat *lots* of 'em. They could eat villagers in one gulp! They were very gifted. But I wouldn't eat villagers. Not one. So everybody said I wasn't a good dragon."

Dang, it must be tough having brothers and sisters, Carlos thought. *I'm glad I'm an only child.*

Pinky looked into Smudge's eyes. She wiped away a stray dragon tear. "You are a good dragon," she said. "And you're a *very* good friend. I'm sorry I yelled at you."

"And I'm sorry I set the boat on fire," Smudge said.

"It's okay," Pinky replied.

Carlos could tell that Pinky meant what she said. It really *was* okay.

"It *is* gonna be okay, Pinky!" Smudge announced. In an instant, he had returned to his old, chipper self. "It's gonna be okay, because we're gonna be rescued!"

"How?" Carlos asked. "By who?"

"The sea monster!"

Smudge pointed. Carlos turned.

A dozen feet away from the sloop's stern, the sea was alive with an angry, churning swirl of sizzling bubbles.

CHAPTER 5

"Oh, no. Oh, no! OH, NO!" Carlos lunged to the edge of the boat and stared down into the water.

The Salty Sea was murky, but Carlos had no trouble spotting the enormous black shape circling the boat.

Pinky joined him at the boat's edge. "Holy crow! Look at the size of that thing," she said. "It's at least a hundred feet long!"

"Yay!" Smudge cheered.

"Smudge! This is nothing to 'yay' about!" Carlos shouted. "Sea monsters eat sailors!"

Smudge pointed to the charred and tattered sail. "Don't worry," he said. "Nobody's gonna think *we're* sailors."

"It's coming up!" Pinky cried.

A black head on a long, snaking neck burst from the water and rose fifty feet into the air. Next to the sea monster, the sloop looked like a bath toy.

"GAAAH!" Carlos and Pinky screamed.

Smudge screamed, too. But his scream sounded different.

"WOW!" Smudge screamed.

The sea monster's forked tongue flickered against the sloop's mast, making the tiny boat bob helplessly sideways.

"GAAAH!" Carlos and Pinky screamed.

"WHEE!" Smudge screamed.

The sea monster studied the sloop's passengers with its cold, yellow eyes. Its mouth opened wide, revealing hundreds of razor-sharp fangs.

"GAAAH!" Carlos and Pinky screamed.

"OH, HAI!" Smudge screamed.

Carlos fell backward onto the deck. He squeezed his eyes shut in terror and waited for the terrible, horrible end.

"OH, HAI!" the sea monster said.

Oh . . . hai? Carlos thought. *Did that thing just say "oh, hai"?*

It did.

"Nice to meet ya in your ocean!" Smudge said, as cheerful as ever. "It is very pleasant. And *wet*! My name is Smudge. I'm a little dragon. This is Pinky. And this is CC. She's a little human, and he is a little human."

"Smudge?" the sea monster asked.

"That's my name! Don't wear it out!" Smudge said.

"Smudge," the sea monster said again. "Smudge. Smuuudge. Smmmmudggggge." The name didn't seem to suit him. "Can I call you Smudge-ickle?" the sea monster asked.

Smudge squeaked with delight. "Smudge-ickle! I *love* that name! Did you hear that, CC? Did you hear my new name? It's Smudge-ickle!"

Carlos pulled himself onto his knees. "I heard." He took a deep, shaky breath. "So. You're not going to eat us, Mr. Sea Monster?"

"Tiny," the sea monster said.

"Tiny?" Carlos said. "Your name is Tiny?"

"What a nice name!" Smudge exclaimed.

"So you're not going to eat us, Tiny?" Carlos asked.

"Oh, no," Tiny said. "I don't eat sailors. I'm here because I saw Smudge-ickle waving. So I wanted to wave back."

So Tiny waved his spiky, scaly tail. "Hai," he said.

"Oh, um, hi," Carlos said.

"So if you don't eat sailors," Smudge asked, "what *do* you eat?"

"Ice cream," Tiny said.

Smudge gasped. "You and me are gonna be bestest friends."

"Wait. You eat ice cream?" Pinky said. "But how . . . ?"

"I know," Tiny replied, "it's hard to find ice cream in the ocean. It's a real problem."

"Maybe we can help you with that," Pinky said. "Have you ever heard of a place called Dessert Island?"

Tiny raised a huge, scaly eyebrow. "No," he admitted. "Is it a nice place?"

"I think you'll like it," she said.

◆　◆　◆

Minutes later, the sloop was tied securely to Tiny's neck.

Moments after that, Tiny was swimming like a sea monster on fire.

"Am I going too fast?" Tiny asked as he zipped through the water. The sloop moved

so quickly that it barely touched the surface. "I don't normally swim this fast, but I also don't normally swim to places where ice cream grows on trees!"

"You're doing great!" Pinky shouted over the wind. She stood on the sloop's

bow, holding a map in one hand and a compass in the other. "Tiny! Go to starboard!"

"Star board?" Tiny asked. "What's a star board?"

"STARBOARD!" Pinky called a little louder. "That means turn right!"

"Gotcha." Tiny did as he was told.

◆　◆　◆

The afternoon sun began to sink in the sky. Tiny had slowed to a less windy speed. Their shadows grew long. The water sparkled like precious jewels. The scene was so beautiful that Carlos, Pinky, and Smudge almost forgot they were on a royal quest. It felt more like a vacation.

Pinky tugged on the rope that tied Tiny to the sloop. Tiny stopped swimming. "Are we almost there?" the sea monster asked.

"Almost," Pinky said, "but let's stop for supper." She reached into the cooler and tossed Tiny a few fudgesickles. He gobbled them up gratefully. Then she pulled out a sandwich for herself. "We'll get started again after nightfall, okay? That way I can navigate by the stars. I've always wanted to try that."

"Navigate by the stars?" Carlos was impressed. "How did you learn to sail?"

Pinky took a bite of sandwich and shrugged. "I ride on lots of boats to paint seascapes. The sailors are always nice. Sometimes they give me sailing lessons."

"Well, you sure know what you're doing," Carlos said. "You really looked heroic up there. I've never seen Gilbert look that heroic."

"Stop teasing me," Pinky replied.

"I'm not teasing you," Carlos protested.

"CC doesn't tease like that, Pinky," Smudge said. "He only teases *brains*."

"Seriously, Pinky," Carlos persisted. "Who's ever heard of anyone steering a sailboat powered by a *sea monster*? That's some cool stuff!"

"I agree," Tiny said. "You looked very cool.

Like the coolest thing ever. Almost as cool as another fudge-ickle."

With a little smile, Pinky dug into the cooler and tossed another fudgesickle to Tiny.

◆　◆　◆

"Do you hear that?" Carlos asked as he took the last bite of his sandwich.

Smudge heard it, too. "Ooh! Pretty!"

Pinky cupped a hand to her ear. "Singing."

"*Pretty* singing," Smudge insisted. "Maybe it's a Broadway musical. Oh, I hope it is. I've always wanted to see that Broadway musical with the cats in it. I don't remember the name of the show, but it has cats!"

"I don't think they put on Broadway shows in the middle of the Salty Sea," Carlos said as he scanned the horizon. "That's weird. I don't see anything."

"Wait. I know where that singing is coming from," Pinky said. She pulled Gilbert's small black journal from her pocket and riffled through it until she found the correct page.

"Mermaids!" she announced.

"Mermaids?" Carlos asked.

"Yes!" Pinky said. "Singing mermaids surround Dessert Island. It says so right here."

Smudge began to hop and skip. "That means we're close to ice cream! And maybe the little mermaids will also put on a Broadway musical about cats!"

"That's great," Carlos said. "The mermaids' voices will lead us straight to Dessert Island."

"Maybe," Pinky said. "But maybe not."

"What do you mean, 'maybe not?'" Carlos asked.

"Well, mermaids sometimes sing to attract sailors," she explained. "And then the mermaids lure those sailors to their doom."

"Doom?" Carlos asked.

Pinky nodded. "Doom. We'll need to proceed with extreme caution."

Smudge, however, was too excited to hear the words *doom* or *extreme* or *caution*. He scampered to the sloop's bow. "TINY!" Smudge shouted. "Swim to the singers as fast as you can! That's where the ice cream is! And the mermaids will maybe put on a Broadway musical!"

"Really?" Tiny asked. "Do you think they'll sing that one with the cats in it?"

"I'm sure of it!" Smudge exclaimed. "LET'S GO!"

And in a rush of churning water, Tiny raced forward as fast as his powerful fins would allow.

CHAPTER 6

"WAIT! WAIT!" Carlos shouted. He used every last ounce of strength to crawl to the bow. The sloop was moving so quickly that the rushing wind kept knocking him off of his feet. "STOP!"

But Tiny was too excited to hear. All he

listened for was the mermaid melodies, which grew louder and louder with each passing second.

The closer they got, the clearer the lyrics became.

If you are sick of cake and scones
And want your tasty treats in cones
Then dock your boat here double-quick
For lotsa flavors you can lick!

Ice cream! Ice cream!
Please listen to our song!
Ice cream! Ice cream!
Lick it all day long!

Our ice cream truly has no peer.

It ain't the best if it ain't here.

So dock your boat and take your seats,

For tasty, neat-o, nifty treats!

Ice cream! Ice cream!

What'cha waiting for?

Ice cream! Ice cream!

Always room for more!

That song is kinda catchy, Carlos thought. *It's a lot better than opera.*

Tiny slowed down, allowing the boat to gently drift past a dozen melodic mermaids lounging on a tiny outcropping of rocks.

Carlos tried not to stare at the mermaids. But he couldn't help himself.

In Carlos's storybooks, mermaids were pretty girls, but instead of legs, they had fish tails.

These mermaids, however, looked a little different.

These mermaids had legs.

And these mermaids had fish heads.

Ice cream! Ice cream!

For every boy and girl!

Ice cream! Ice cream!

Eat up until you hurl!

"I will do that, little mermaids!" Smudge exclaimed. "I will do *exactly* that!"

Smudge turned to Carlos. "Wow, CC," the dragon whispered. "Mermaids are even prettier than they are in the storybooks!"

"Excuse us!" Pinky called out. "Are you the Dessert Island mermaids?"

"Those aren't mermaids," Tiny said. "They're *more*maids."

"*More*maids?" Pinky asked.

"Mermaids are half fish and half maiden," Tiny explained, "but these young ladies only have fish heads. They're, like, eighty-five percent maiden. So they're more-maids."

The moremaids nodded their fish heads in agreement.

"Do moremaids lead sailors to their doom?" Carlos asked.

"No," Tiny replied. "They lead sailors to ice cream. I thought that was obvious."

"Excuse me, moremaids," Pinky said. "Could you help us? We're looking for someone."

"We're also looking for ice cream," Smudge said.

"*Lots* of ice cream," Tiny said.

"Yes, that, too," Pinky admitted. "But we need to find a person. A prince. Has any prince come this way in the last few weeks?"

The moremaids silently considered this for a moment. They replied in three-part harmony.

Three weeks ago, he came ashore.

He didn't know what was in store.

But now he does, and what is more:

Our tasty treat is Gilbert's chore!

Ice cream! Ice cream!

We'll lead you to your friend.

Ice cream! Ice cream!

Come if you comprehend.

"What are they talking about?" Pinky muttered.

"I may be wrong," Carlos replied, "but I think they just gave us a brainteaser."

Pinky groaned. "Oh, no. Not another one of those. So what's the answer?"

"I don't know yet," Carlos said.

"Do you think it means they're going to put on that Broadway show with the cats in it?" Smudge asked.

"No, I don't," Carlos said.

Carlos closed his eyes in concentration. "Excuse me? Mermaids?"

"*More*maids," Tiny corrected.

"Oh, right. *More*maids. Sorry," Carlos said. "Could you please sing that song again? But a little slower this time?"

The moremaids nodded their fish heads and sang.

Three weeks ago, he came ashore.

He didn't know what was in store.

But now he does, and what is more:

Our tasty treat is Gilbert's chore.

"Holy schmoley! I figured it out!" Carlos exclaimed.

"It's a brainteaser about food!" Smudge exclaimed. "I figured it out, too!"

Carlos and Smudge shouted the correct answer together: "Gilbert is working in the Dessert Island ice cream store!"

CHAPTER 7

Instead of armor, he wore a striped apron. Instead of a crown, he wore a paper hat. Instead of a confident, gleaming smile, he wore a frown, and his lower lip quivered.

He stood alone behind a long, gleaming counter, hunched over a forty-gallon barrel of mixed rainbow sprinkles. Resting on the counter were dozens of tall sprinkle piles. Each sprinkle pile was a different color.

Gilbert held a pair of tweezers. Using the tweezers, he plucked a single sprinkle from the barrel. With great care, he placed the sprinkle on the correctly colored sprinkle pile.

He did this over and over and over again.

When the store's front door jingled open, he didn't bother looking up from his work. "Welcome to the Dessert Island Ice Cream-ery of Creamy Concoctions," he said in a distracted monotone. "It is my royal honor to serve you."

"Gilbert?" Pinky said.

Gilbert turned to the door. An expression of horror swept across his face. "Oh, no," he cried. "Oh, no no no no no!" Gilbert covered his face with his hands. "I'm not who you

think I am! You've mistaken me for someone else!

But it *wasn't* someone else. It was Gilbert.
Though never in Carlos's life had he seen
Gilbert look so . . . *un-Gilberty*.

"What the heck happened to you?" Pinky
asked.

"Are you okay?" Carlos asked.

"Can I have a milkshake?" Smudge asked.

Gilbert answered the questions in order:
"Long story. No. What flavor?"

"What flavors do you have?" Smudge
asked.

"We have two thousand and twelve ice
cream flavors," Gilbert said.

"What are they?" Smudge asked.

"Smudge, we'll order ice cream in a couple of minutes, okay?" Carlos said. "Talk to us, Gilbert. Why are you here?"

"Because I can't go home," Gilbert said.

Pinky rolled her eyes. "Of *course* you can go home! We talked to those people with the fish heads. You're not being held prisoner."

"That's not the reason why I can't go home," Gilbert said.

"And we saw your boat," Pinky continued. "It looks fine. So we know you weren't shipwrecked."

"That's not the reason, either." Gilbert turned his attention back to the sprinkles.

"Stop that! Stop doing that thing with the sprinkles!" Pinky lunged for Gilbert's tweezers, but Gilbert was too fast for her. "Why on earth are you tweezing sprinkles?"

"Because they come off the sprinkle trees all mixed up," Gilbert explained. "And many customers prefer un-rainbowed sprinkles. Look, I don't have to explain myself to you! The reason I'm here is none of your business." Gilbert plucked a blue sprinkle from the barrel and carefully moved it to the blue sprinkle pile on the counter. "You wouldn't understand, anyway."

"What did you say?" Pinky put her hands on her hips. "I wouldn't *understand*?"

"No," Gilbert said. "You wouldn't."

"Try me," Pinky said.

"No," Gilbert said.

"Tell me or you'll regret it," Pinky said.

"No," Gilbert said.

"You will *really* regret it," Pinky said.

"No," Gilbert said.

"Fine!" Pinky shouted. She swept her arms across the counter, sending jillions of neatly ordered sprinkles skipping, skittering, and scattering in every direction.

"NOOOOOO!" Gilbert howled.

"Regret stinks," Pinky said.

Dang. I'm really *glad I'm an only child*, Carlos thought.

"Don't worry, Gert!" Smudge announced. "I will clean up your delicious sprinkles!"

Pinky stared hard at Gilbert, her dark eyes as cold as steel. "Now tell me what's going on or I'll give you *another* regret! You *know* I can do it, Gilbert!"

"All right!" Gilbert held his hands up in surrender. "I'll tell you."

"Why can't you go home?" she asked.

"Because . . ." Gilbert paused. It was difficult for him to say. "Because I failed my royal quest."

This news was greeted with a long silence.

"And . . . ?" Pinky asked.

"And nothing," Gilbert said. "That's the reason."

"*That's* the reason?" she asked.

"YES!" Gilbert shouted so loudly, his paper hat fell off. "That's the reason I can't go back! Ever-After Land was counting on me! Every kingdom on the continent was waiting for me to return in triumph! I was going to get a bronze statue in Ever-After

Square! My birthday was going to be a national holiday! The Ever-After Deli was going to name a cheese sandwich after me!"

"They were going to do all that for you?" Pinky asked.

"I don't know. Maybe," Gilbert said. "But it doesn't matter. I found the Be-Sworded Stone. It's just a short walk from here. But I can't get the sword out of it! I've tried a million times. And every time I've tried, I've failed! I've *failed*!"

"So you failed! So what?" Pinky said. "Geez, Gilbert! Everybody has to fail at something sometimes."

"Not me," Gilbert said.

"Yes, you!" Pinky grabbed the front of Gilbert's apron and tried to shake some sense into him. "What makes you so ding-dang special? *Everybody* fails, dummy!"

Gilbert swatted her hands away. "I *know* everybody fails, but . . ." He sighed a very unhappy sigh. "But nobody ever expects *me* to fail."

Gilbert looked away. That was when he noticed Smudge. As promised, the dragon was cleaning up the spilled sprinkles. To be more accurate, Smudge was *licking* up the spilled sprinkles. Jillions and jillions of them.

The licking was gross and slimy and unsanitary, but Gilbert was too depressed to do anything about it.

He turned back to Pinky. "For my whole

life—for my *entire* life—everyone has expected me to be perfect. Always perfect," Gilbert said. "And trying to be perfect all the time is just so . . . so . . ."

Pinky completed his thought. "Poop stinky?"

Gilbert nodded.

"You *have* to go back." Pinky's angry, impatient tone was long gone now; it was replaced with something far gentler. "Everybody misses you."

"Everybody misses Gilbert the *perfect*. They're not going to be too worried about Gilbert the *failure*."

"*I'm* worried about Gilbert the failure," Pinky admitted.

"You are?" he asked.

"Yeah," she said. "Come home with us. It's okay not to be perfect, Gilbert. It's okay to fail. Really."

Gilbert considered this for a long time.

"Maybe it's okay to fail at *little* things," he said. "But a *royal quest*? That's a *big* deal." He shook his head. "It's *too* big a deal. I can't fail that. I'm not going back."

He adjusted his apron. "And this job isn't so bad. It's not bad at all. So I'm going to stay right here, safe and sound, blending milkshakes." He turned to Smudge. "How about a chocolate milkshake? The chocolate here is very good."

"No, thank you," the dragon groaned. His belly gurgled and churned. "I think I cleaned up too many sprinkles."

CHAPTER 8

As Pinky took Smudge to Dessert Island's first aid station, Carlos and Gilbert walked to the beach. The sun had started to set. The sky was alive with pink and orange streaks.

Dessert Island was one of the most beautiful places Carlos had ever seen. To their left, the crystal-clear surf gently lapped against the white sand. To their right, a long row of flowering trees stood tall and straight. Frosty balls of cookies 'n' cream and butter-pecan ice cream dangled from their branches.

"These trees are amazing," Gilbert said. "Each tree grows a freezer unit inside of its trunk. That's why the ice cream stays cold in warm weather."

Carlos wasn't really listening. His mind was a million miles away.

"Rocky road is in season," Gilbert went on. "And I'm going to harvest the waffle cones tomorrow morning."

"Where is it?" Carlos asked.

"Where's what?" Gilbert asked. "The waffle cones?"

Carlos shook his head. "The Be-Sworded Stone."

"Oh," Gilbert replied. "Just over the hill."

Carlos didn't know what the Be-Sworded Stone looked like, but he assumed it would be impressive. He imagined a mountain of shining white marble. He imagined the sword to be made of solid, glittering gold.

Nope.

Not even close.

The Be-Sworded Stone was just a rock—an ugly gray one no higher than his waist. Sticking out of the rock was the sword. The sword was ugly and gray, too. And crooked.

"This is *it*?" Carlos asked.

Gilbert nodded.

Carlos ran his fingers over the words roughly scratched into the rock's side:

Whosoever discovers the sword in the Be-Sworded Stone and takes it home will bring endless joy to his or her kingdom!

"So this is the royal quest?" Carlos asked.

"Yes," Gilbert said.

"But you can't complete this royal quest, so you're not going home," Carlos said.

"Yes," Gilbert repeated, a little sadder this time.

"What if I do it for you?" Carlos asked.

Gilbert raised a suspicious eyebrow. "Do what?"

Carlos carefully eyed the sword. "What if I completed this royal quest for you?"

Gilbert let out a short, unhappy chuckle. "You can't."

"What if I can?" Carlos persisted. "What if I complete the royal quest *and* I let you take credit for it? Would you come home then?"

Gilbert folded his arm across his chest. "This is a silly discussion."

"What's silly about it? What would you do if I completed this quest and gave you all the credit?" Carlos leapt upon the rock. "And I won't just *give* you credit. I'll *announce* it! I will scream from the rooftops, 'GILBERT THE GALLANT COMPLETED THE

ROYAL QUEST! GIVE HIM THE CREDIT HE DESERVES! NAME A CHEESE SANDWICH AFTER THAT MAN!'"

"Are you done teasing me?" Gilbert asked.

Carlos clambered down from the rock. "I'm not teasing you. I'm just asking you a question. If I complete this quest and give you the credit, will you go home with us?"

Gilbert turned away. "I'm going back to sort sprinkles."

"Hey!" Carlos shouted. "This is important!"

"No, Carlos, this is *not* important!" Gilbert shouted back. "Because you will never,

ever be able to get that sword out of that stone!"

"I know that," Carlos said. "It's impossible." Carlos placed his hand on the sword's handle. "It's impossible because *this sword isn't a sword at all.*"

That got Gilbert's attention.

"It's a stone sculpture," Carlos continued. "This sword was *carved* from this big, ugly rock."

"WHAT?!" Gilbert raced back to the Be-Sworded Stone. He studied the sword closely. "Oh, my goodness! You're right! Both the stone and the sword are a single piece of rock!"

"That's why you couldn't pull it out," Carlos said.

Gilbert shook his head in confusion. "But I don't understand! If no one can pull out the sword, how can anyone complete the royal quest?"

"The royal quest is a brainteaser," Carlos explained. He read the inscription aloud. "'Whosoever discovers the sword in the Be-Sworded Stone and takes it home will bring endless joy to his or her king-dom!'"

Gilbert looked at Carlos blankly. He still didn't get it.

"The inscription doesn't say anything

about taking the sword *out* of the stone," Carlos said.

Gilbert read the passage again. "Holy crow! It doesn't!"

Carlos smiled. "To complete this royal quest, all you need to do is take this big, ugly rock home."

CHAPTER 9

Two thousand and twelve ice cream scoops later, Tiny was ready to give everyone a ride back to the far shore of Ever-After Land, across the Salty Sea. The moremaids tied the battered sloop and Gilbert's boat together. (The two boats were just big enough to support the weight of the Be-Sworded Stone.) Pinky tied the boats to Tiny's neck.

"I can't believe it," Gilbert marveled. "You guys made friends with a sea monster? That is very heroic!"

"And very cool," Tiny added. "Sea monsters are always cool. What's your name, stranger?"

"Prince Gilbert," said Gilbert.

"Gilbert? Gillllllberrrrt. Giiiiiiillllllllll-beeeeeeeerrrrrrt. Hm." Tiny twisted his mouth into a thoughtful grimace. "Can I call you Gilb-ickle?"

"I'd rather you didn't," Gilbert said.

"Gilb-ickle." Tiny nodded. As far as he was concerned, the matter was settled.

"Gilb-ickle! What a great name!" Smudge exclaimed. The dragon still had a bellyache from eating all those sprinkles, but he was in good spirits anyway.

"Full speed ahead!" Pinky announced.

Tiny did as he was told.

◆ ◆ ◆

Word traveled fast in Ever-After Land. As soon as Tiny and the boats peeked over the horizon, church bells began ringing.

Marching bands assembled. Town criers shouted the news from every village square:

"GILBERT HAS RETURNED FROM HIS ROYAL QUEST! GILBERT THE GAL-LANT IS HOME!"

By the time the boats crunched against the sandy shore, a huge, joyous, chanting crowd was there to meet them.

"Gil-BERT! Gil-BERT! Gil-BERT!" the crowd yelled.

"Incredible," Pinky grumbled under her breath.

It *was* incredible. Carlos finally began to understand just how hard it was to have Gilbert for a brother. Without thinking, Carlos put his arm around Pinky's shoulders and gave her a gentle squeeze.

Gilbert triumphantly leapt onto the Be-Sworded Stone. He held up his hands to silence the crowd, but the crowd wasn't ready

GIL-BERT! GIL-BERT!

to be quiet. Their perfect prince had re-turned! They *needed* to cheer, long and loud.

"Thank you for this warm and wonderful greeting!" Gilbert said over the roar. He smiled his perfect smile. "It is wonderful to finally be home!"

"Gil-BERT! Gil-BERT! Gil-BERT!"

Again, Gilbert put up a silencing hand. "I had quite an adventure! Would you like to hear about it?"

The crowd whistled and whooped with delight. If there was one thing the people of Ever-After Land loved, it was a good adventure story. And Gilbert was a perfect storyteller.

Pinky whispered into Carlos's ear, "Do you think he'll give us any credit at all?"

Carlos shook his head. "I told him to take all the credit."

"What?" Pinky's eyes blazed. "Why would you tell him to do that?"

"He needs the credit more than we do. A lot more," Carlos said. "I'm a jester prince. You're an artist princess. But Gilbert is *just* a prince. That's all he has. Royal quests don't matter to us. But they mean *everything* to him."

Pinky considered this. She nodded. "Yeah, you're right."

"Besides," Carlos said, "*we* know what we did."

"We sure do," Pinky said.

Pinky and Carlos turned their attention back to the cheering crowd. Only then did they notice that the chant had changed:

"Pink-Y! Car-LOS! Pink-Y! Car-LOS!"

"Whoa. What happened?" Pinky whispered.

Carlos turned to Gilbert. The perfect prince was smiling from ear to ear.

"Come on! You can do better than that!" Gilbert called out to the crowd. "Prince

Carlos completed my royal quest! I *failed*! But *he* succeeded!"

"WOOO!" went the crowd.

"And my wonderful sister, Princess Pinky, tamed a sea monster and led an expedition to Dessert Island. And then she rescued me. She rescued me in more ways than one."

As the crowd went wild, Gilbert reached out to Pinky and gave her a big hug. She hugged him back.

"Thank you, you big failure," she said.

"That's the nicest thing anyone has ever said to me," Gilbert replied.

Gilbert reached out to shake Carlos's

hand. Carlos leaned toward Gilbert's ear. "Why didn't you take credit for the royal quest? That was the deal."

"Accepting that deal would have been unprincely," Gilbert said. "I may not be a perfect prince, but I am a *princely* prince."

"You certainly are," Carlos agreed. And he meant it.

◆ ◆ ◆

Gilbert insisted that the Be-Sworded Stone belonged to Faraway Kingdom.

"You solved the riddle," Gilbert told Carlos. "You deserve the glory."

So it was placed in Faraway Kingdom's village square. The people paid attention to the Be-Sworded Stone for a little while. The village children tugged at the sword for a day or two. But it didn't take long for everyone to sort of forget that it was there.

Except for Carlos and Smudge.

"Dang, that rock is ugly," Carlos said.

"And it is a liar," Smudge harrumphed.

"What do you mean?" Carlos asked.

Smudge pointed a sharp, black talon at the inscription and read it aloud: "'Whosoever discovers the sword in the Be-Sworded Stone and takes it home will bring endless joy to his or her kingdom!'"

Carlos shrugged. "So?"

"So the rock says we should be getting *endless joy*!" Smudge said. "Did you get endless joy?"

"Endless joy? No," Carlos admitted.

"I'm a pretty joyful dragon," Smudge said. "But my joyfulness has not been *endless*! So this rock lied to us! It *lied*!"

Carlos nodded. The rock *did* sort of lie.

"Can I kick it?" Smudge asked.

"You want to kick the rock?"

"Just a little kick," Smudge said, "for being such a liar of a rock."

Carlos gave the dragon a little salute. "Sure, go wild."

Smudge didn't need to be told twice.

THWACK!

It wasn't a big kick, but it was big enough.

The rock cracked.

"Uh-oh," Smudge said.

The crack grew.

"Oh, no!" Smudge cried.

And the rock split open.

Smudge began to panic. "I am so sorry, CC! But it's not my fault! You said I could kick it! You *said* I could!"

"Relax," Carlos said. "It's okay. Look. The rock is hollow."

The split was only a couple of inches wide. Carlos peeked inside. He couldn't see much, but he did see *something*.

He carefully reached his hand inside and pulled out a small sphere about the size of a marble. It was green with small black flecks. He and Smudge stared at it for a long time.

"What is it?" Smudge asked.

"I don't know." Carlos let the sphere roll around in his palm. The texture was smooth.

Smudge reached into the rock and pulled out more spheres. A big pawful. They were all the same size, but every one was a different color.

"There are lots of 'em in there," Smudge said. "Hundreds, maybe."

Carlos brought the sphere up to his nose and sniffed.

"Thousands," Carlos replied. "Two thousand and twelve to be exact."

"How do you know that?" Smudge asked.

But before Smudge finished asking the

question, he knew the answer. Smudge had a talent for brainteasers about food.

The dragon pointed to Carlos's sphere. "Chocolate-chip mint?"

Carlos gave Smudge a huge, knowing smile.

"ICE CREAM TREE SEEDS!" Smudge squealed. "AT LAST! ENDLESS JOY!"

ABOUT THE AUTHOR

Roy L. Hinuss is the authorized biographer of the Charming Royal Family. He is also fond of the occasional fart joke. When he isn't writing about Prince Carlos Charles Charming's many adventures, he pursues his life's goal to create a tree that makes Brussels sprout ice cream.